Julie Andrews Edwards & Emma Walton Hamilton

Dumpy
at School

Illustrated by Tony Walton

Hyperion Books for Children/New York

"**COCK-A-DOODLE-DOO!**" crowed the rooster on the barn roof at Merryhill Farm. (He does it every morning.)

"**BEEP! BEEP! BEEP!**"

Dumpy peered sleepily through the barn doors and saw Farmer Barnes loading Bee-Bee the Backhoe onto a huge trailer. Suddenly he remembered why today was special: he and Bee-Bee had both been hired to do their first real job away from the farm. His radiator felt full of bubbles as he wondered what it would be like to work on a real construction site.

Up at the farmhouse, Charlie Barnes was waking up, too.

His grandfather, Pop-Up, poked his head around the bedroom door.

"Time to get up, pal! We don't want to be late for your first day of school!"

Charlie felt his stomach flutter as he wondered what the day would bring, and whether he would make any friends. Then the tempting smell of Mom's special French toast drifted up the stairs, so he hurried into his new clothes.

Pop-Up was already at the breakfast table, enjoying a steaming cup of tea. Charlie slid into the seat beside him and noticed a shiny lunch box sitting on his place mat.

"A lunch box with Dumpy on it!" he exclaimed. "Where did you find it?"

"I bought it at Pharaoh's General Store," said Mrs. Barnes, "but the picture was just an ordinary dump truck, until Pop-Up borrowed your paints and made it look like *our* Dumpy."

Pop-Up winked at Charlie.

"Speaking of Dumpy, I'd better go get him out of the barn and warm up his engine. We've *all* got a big day ahead! Remember, he's going to school today, too."

Charlie finished his breakfast and wriggled into his backpack.

"Have a *terrific* day," his mother whispered, giving him a big hug.

"**BRROOM! BRROOM!**" Dumpy pulled up to the back porch, towing Bee-Bee on her trailer behind him.

"Hop in, pal!" said Pop-Up, at the wheel.

Charlie blew a kiss to his mom and
waved to his dad, who was working with
Trundle the Tractor across the field.
"**PUTT-PUTT-PUTT-PUTT!**" said
Trundle as he turned over the brown earth.
"All in a day's work!"

It was a sparkling autumn morning.

Pop-Up glanced at Charlie. "You're very quiet, pal," he said.
"Got butterflies in your tummy?"

Charlie nodded.

"Very normal for your first day at school," Pop-Up reassured him. "I'll bet Dumpy feels just as nervous as you do."

"**BRROOOM! BRROOOM!** . . ." Dumpy agreed softly, and his engine missed a beat. Building a bigger playground for the school would be much harder than his everyday chores on the farm.

They pulled into the school yard just as Steady Gus the School Bus arrived.

"HONKETY-HONK!" called Steady Gus. Red lights flashing merrily, he added, "Safety first!"

As the double doors hissed open and children tumbled out, Charlie's heart sank.

"What if they think I'm weird arriving at school in a dump truck?" he asked.

"Pshaw!" said Pop-Up. "They should be so lucky! And when they see the new playground, they'll *all* want to ride Dumpy to school. Now, off you go, pal. We'll see you at two o'clock."

"Good morning, boys and girls!" Mrs. Bundle, the schoolteacher, greeted them. "Hang up your coats, then come sit on the big red rug and we'll introduce ourselves."

Charlie felt his throat tighten. He hoped he wouldn't be first to speak.

"My name is Isabelle," said one little girl.

"Joey Scavullo," said the boy next to her.

"Sam David Wells, the third," said another boy, with glasses.

The others spoke up, too— Max, Hannah, Jake, Maggie, Joelie, Georgia, Maisie, Molly . . .

"Charlie . . ." said Charlie, in a whisper.

Mrs. Bundle smiled encouragingly.

"Well, we're off to a good start! Now, who's got something for show-and-tell?"

Outside the school, as Pop-Up unloaded Bee-Bee from the trailer, Dumpy stared in awe at the large hill in front of him. How would he ever move all that earth?

GRRRRRACKLE-CRACKLE-CRUNCH-STOMP!

The ground shook beneath him, and a huge yellow-and-black monster machine loomed into view.

"STAND ASIDE!" it roared. "I'm comin' through."

Pop-Up saluted the driver.

"Thought we were going to have to do the whole job ourselves," he joked. "Should've known Buzz the Bulldozer wouldn't let us down!"

Dumpy's tires sagged a little. He suddenly felt very small.

"**BEEP! BEEP! BEEP!**" Bee-Bee pulled up beside him. "Two hands are better than one. . . ." she said kindly.

"Lunchtime!" Mrs. Bundle announced.

Charlie pulled out his new lunch box. He wondered how Dumpy and Pop-Up were doing.

"What's in *your* sandwich?" asked Joey.

"Peanut butter and banana," Charlie replied.

"Trade ya!" Joey shoved his tuna on rye under Charlie's nose. Charlie hesitated, then gave away his favorite lunch.

"Hi! I'm Molly." A friendly brown-haired girl sat down beside him. "Want to share?" She held out a bagel filled with cream cheese and jelly.

"It's tuna fish," Charlie said.

"Oh. Never mind!" Molly moved away to join Hannah at the next table.

Charlie sighed.

All morning long Dumpy had raced back and forth, taking load after load of earth from the playground to the local garden center.

But as fast as he went, Buzz went faster. He leveled the ground in no time, taking tree stumps and rocks in his stride. Bee-Bee was always ready and waiting to fill Dumpy's bed with another load that seemed bigger than the last. Dumpy's lifting arm was sore, and he felt hot and cranky.

At recess, the children rushed to peer over the orange fencing. They had eyes only for Buzz. Charlie alone hung back from the crowd of admirers and came over to comfort Dumpy.

"Never mind, Dumpy," he said. "You're still the best."

Classes finally ended, and the school bell rang. Children laughed
and chattered as they clambered aboard Steady Gus.

Pop-Up folded Charlie in a big hug.

"Did you have a good day, pal?"

Charlie nodded, then shrugged his shoulders.

"I think Dumpy had a hard time, too," whispered Pop-Up.

"But each day will get easier," said Mrs. Bundle.

Pop-Up tipped his hat. "Good afternoon, Rosemary." He smiled.

"**ERRR . . . ERRR . . . ERRR . . .**" Steady Gus was suddenly making unusual noises. "**CLACKETY-GAK! WHEEZE! HACK!**"

"Oh dear," Mrs. Bundle called to the bus driver. "What is it, Stanley?"

"**ERRR . . . ERRR . . . ERRR . . .**" Steady Gus sputtered and coughed. "**HISS! BOING! THUD!**"

Stanley slowly descended from the bus, scratching his head.

"I *think* we have a problem. . . ." he said.

"What are we to do?" Mrs. Bundle worried. "How will the children get home?"

Everyone was silent.

"**BRROOOM! BRROOOM!**" Dumpy's headlights flashed in the sun.

"Hey!" cried Charlie suddenly. "Let's take everyone home in Dumpy!"

"But is it safe?" said Mrs. Bundle.

"Perfectly!" Pop-Up boasted. "We'll putter along at ten miles per hour, and our Dumpy will protect his precious passengers from every pothole."

"**BRROOOM, BRROOOM** . . ." agreed Dumpy softly.

"*Well*, then," said Mrs. Bundle, "in that case, all aboard Dumpy."

"YAY!" The children shouted.
"WOW! This is *yours*?" said Joey
Scavullo. "This is totally GREAT!"
Charlie smiled proudly.
Dumpy carefully rolled out of the school
yard, "**BEEP***!*"-ing hello to Tommy the Tow
Truck, who was on his way in to collect
Steady Gus.

"**CHUGGA-CHUGGA-CHUG!**" said Tommy. "When they're *down*, I pick 'em *up*!"

"Hold on tight, children!" said Mrs. Bundle. "Let's sing a song!"

Dumpy made his way slowly and triumphantly through Apple Harbor, Bee-Bee on her trailer bringing up the rear.

People stopped to wave and admire the unusual sight of the brightly colored convoy and a dump truck filled with children, singing at the tops of their voices.

"Hooray for Dumpy!" they all yelled.

Pop-Up drove proudly, his hat on the back of his head.

"Even the mighty Buzz couldn't have done *this*," he said softly to Dumpy.

"**BRROOOM! BRROOOM!**" Dumpy roared, and joined in the song with a "**TOOT!**" in just the right key.

Singing loudest of all was Charlie. He was surrounded by new friends . . . and he knew that from now on, school was going to be *fun*.

For Hannah, Isabelle, Max, Georgia, Joelie, Bingham, and, of course, *Sam*.

Printed in the United States of America
This book is set in 19-point Colwell.
The artwork for each picture was prepared using watercolor and colored pencil.

FIRST EDITION
1 3 5 7 9 10 8 6 4 2

Library of Congress Cataloging-in-Publication Data

Edwards, Julie, 1935–
Dumpy at school / by Julie Andrews Edwards and Emma Walton Hamilton ;
illustrated by Tony Walton.—1st ed.
p. cm.
Summary: Charlie, who is nervous about his first day of school, and
Dumpy the Dump Truck, who is nervous about his first construction job,
gradually adjust to their new settings after making new friends.
ISBN 0-7868-0610-9
[1. First day of school—Fiction. 2. Schools—Fiction. 3. Dump trucks—Fiction.
4. Trucks—Fiction.] I. Hamilton, Emma Walton. II. Walton, Tony, ill. III. Title.

PZ7.E2562 Dp 2000   [E]—dc21
00-026863

Visit www.hyperionchildrensbooks.com